STAR WARS

MEET THE
GALACTIC VILLAINS

WRITTEN BY EMELI JUHLIN

ART BY TITMOUSE AND TOMATOFARM

PRESS

Los Angeles • New York

A long time ago
in a galaxy far, far away,
there were brave heroes
and sinister villains.

The heroes came together
to protect the galaxy from Sith,
gangsters, and bounty hunters.
Some of those heroes were Jedi.

The Jedi use the Force for good.
The Force is an energy field
that connects all living things.

Some villains use the Force for evil.
They are known as Sith.
The Sith study the dark side.

Darth Maul is a Sith.
He is a student of a Sith Lord
named Darth Sidious.
They want to rule the galaxy.

Darth Maul wants to stop the Jedi.
He fights a Jedi named Qui-Gon Jinn.
Qui-Gon protects a young boy
named Anakin Skywalker.

Qui-Gon wants Anakin
to study the Force.
When Darth Maul defeats Qui-Gon,
Obi-Wan Kenobi fights Darth Maul.

Anakin grows up and
becomes Obi-Wan's Padawan.
A Padawan is a student who
trains in the ways of the Force.

Obi-Wan and Anakin fight Sith
like Count Dooku.
Dooku wants to start a war.
Obi-Wan and Anakin must stop him.

Dooku is too strong.
Master Yoda, a small and wise Jedi,
comes to help them.
Dooku escapes!

The Sith Lord Darth Sidious
uses Force lightning.
After Maul and Dooku are defeated,
Sidious takes Anakin as his student.

Sidious trains Anakin
in the ways of the dark side.
Anakin lets his anger control him
and gives in to his fear.

Obi-Wan wants to save Anakin,
but it is too late.
Anakin has turned to the dark side.
He becomes Darth Vader.

Darth Vader commands the armies
of the Galactic Empire.
The armies are made up of
soldiers known as stormtroopers.

Darth Vader will stop at nothing
until he defeats his former master.
Obi-Wan believes he has lost
his friend to the dark side forever.

Years later, Darth Vader captures
Princess Leia of Alderaan.
She has the plans for the Death Star,
the Empire's superweapon.

Jabba the Hutt is a slimy gangster who lives on the planet Tatooine. Many people owe Jabba money.

Han Solo owes Jabba money.
Obi-Wan and Luke Skywalker
hire Han to help them rescue Leia.

Luke wants to be a Jedi.
He hopes Obi-Wan will train him.
But when Vader captures them,
Obi-Wan lets Vader defeat him.

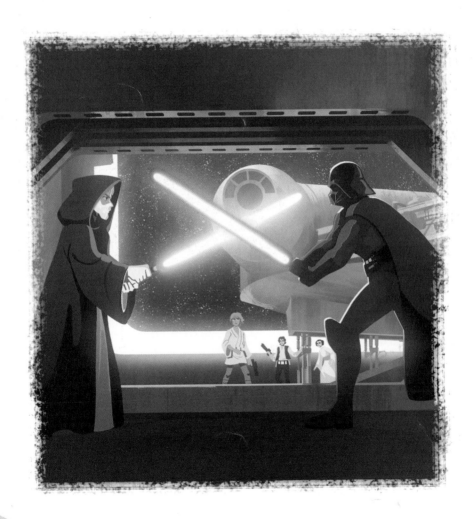

Thanks to Obi-Wan,
the others are able to escape.
Darth Vader hires a bounty hunter
named Boba Fett to catch them again.

Boba takes Han back to Jabba.
At the same time, Luke arrives
and confronts Darth Vader.

Darth Vader wants Luke to join him and turn to the dark side.
Luke escapes from Vader!

Luke and Vader battle
for a second time.
But Luke will not give in to his anger.
He knows Vader can still be good.

Darth Sidious attacks Luke
with Force lightning.
Vader saves Luke!
Vader becomes Anakin again.

Years later, an evil group called
the First Order replaces the Empire.
Kylo Ren follows in the footsteps
of Darth Vader and becomes a leader.
He commands the First Order armies.

Kylo meets Rey.

Rey is part of the Resistance.

She is strong in the Force.

Kylo wants to stop the Resistance.

Rey wants to stop the First Order.

On the planet Crait,
the Resistance is in trouble.
The First Order attacks their base!
Kylo becomes even angrier
when he sees Luke.

Luke has come to face Kylo.
While Luke and Kylo battle,
the heroes escape.
Luke remembers when he faced Vader.
He knows Kylo can still be good.

When Rey confronts Darth Sidious,
Kylo turns to the light side.
They face Darth Sidious together.

Rey destroys Darth Sidious
once and for all.
She helps defeat the First Order!

These are the sinister villains
from a galaxy far, far away.
They have been defeated by
the brave heroes . . . for now!